The Happiest Hippo

in the World

JJ
STEEL

For Nicky,
with all my heart and love
forever.

This story was written for him many, many years ago. I read it to him
every night and he loved it, because Nicky was different too.

And to Sebastian, Isabel, Daisy, Johnny, and Delphina.
With all my love
—D.S.

To Ken and Matt, with all my love
—M.S.

The Happiest Hippo in the World
Text copyright © 2009 by Danielle Steel
Illustrations copyright © 2009 by Margaret Spengler

Manufactured in China.

Library of Congress Cataloging-in-Publication Data is available.
ISBN 978-0-06-157899-1 (trade bdg.)

Designed by Stephanie Bart-Horvath
09 10 11 12 13 SCP 10 9 8 7 6 5 4 3 2 1
❖
First Edition

The Happiest Hippo in the World

by Danielle Steel

illustrated by Margaret Spengler

HarperCollins *Publishers*

nce upon a time, there was a great big gray mother hippopotamus. She lived in the circus with an even bigger great big gray father hippo and several gray hippo children.

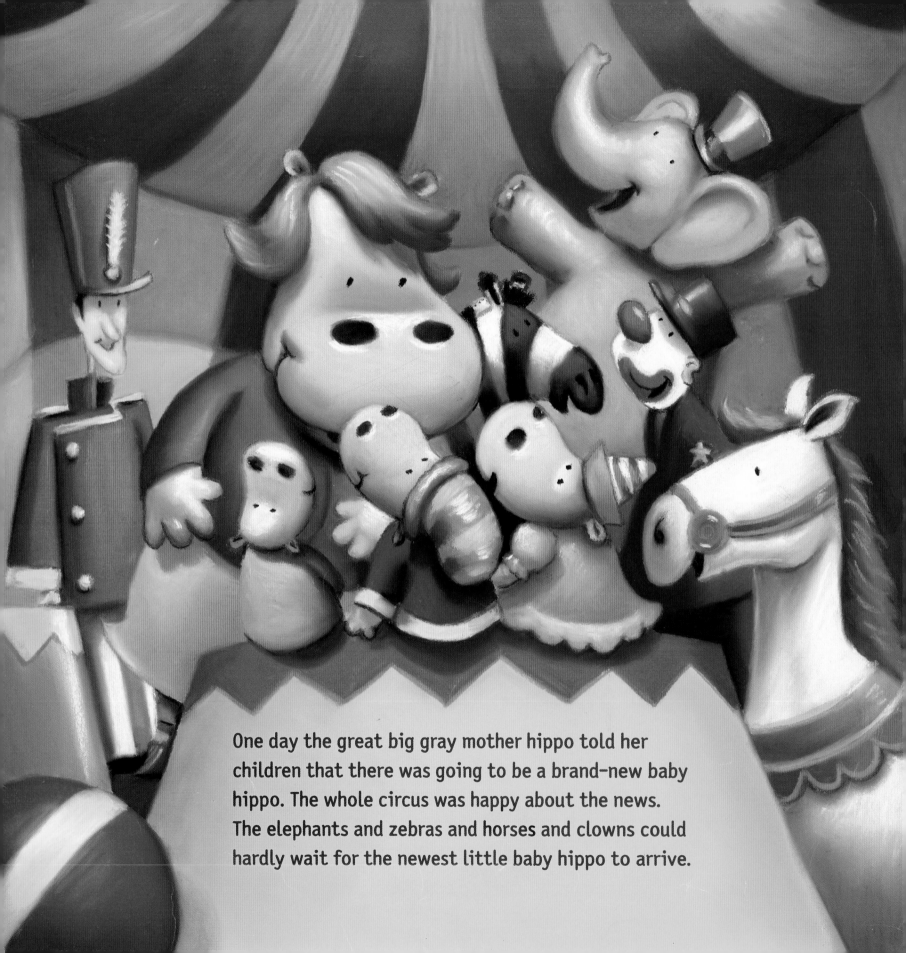

One day the great big gray mother hippo told her children that there was going to be a brand-new baby hippo. The whole circus was happy about the news. The elephants and zebras and horses and clowns could hardly wait for the newest little baby hippo to arrive.

The clowns were especially excited and had plans to dress up the new hippo in baby clothes and drive it around in their clown car.

Finally, the new baby arrived. It was a boy! Mama Hippo was so excited to see him for the first time. But then she realized something strange. She closed her eyes and opened them again and saw the same thing: Her new little hippo was not gray. He was green! A bright, shiny, beautiful emerald green!

Now, there are many things that are green. Grass, leaves, four-leaf clovers, lettuce. But not hippos. Hippos are supposed to be gray.

"What happened?" asked Father Hippo. "Do you think you ate too much spinach before he was born?" All the hippo brothers and sisters thought it was very funny, except the littlest sister, who was a bit scared.

Pretty soon the whole circus knew that the new baby hippo was green. Everyone could tell he was very sweet, but there was no denying that he was very different.

Mama and Father Hippo named the new baby Alphonse, but no one ever called him that. They just called him Greenie, and he called himself that too.

Greenie traveled with the rest of the circus, but he found that life on the road wasn't so easy. Not only was he a green hippo, but he was also huge.

Absolutely
huge!

Children thought that Greenie looked scary. He was just too different from all the other animals and all the other hippos. He was even different from his own family.

The owner of the circus decided that the circus just wasn't the right place for Greenie. He was too big, too green, and just too different.

So Greenie said good-bye to the circus and took the train to New York City. He wanted to find a place where he would fit in. Surely there had to be other green hippopotamuses somewhere, and Greenie was sure he'd find them in New York.

New York was a little scary for him at first. The buildings were very tall, and there were a lot of people and noises (like cars and taxis honking). And then one day, he found Central Park when he was out walking.

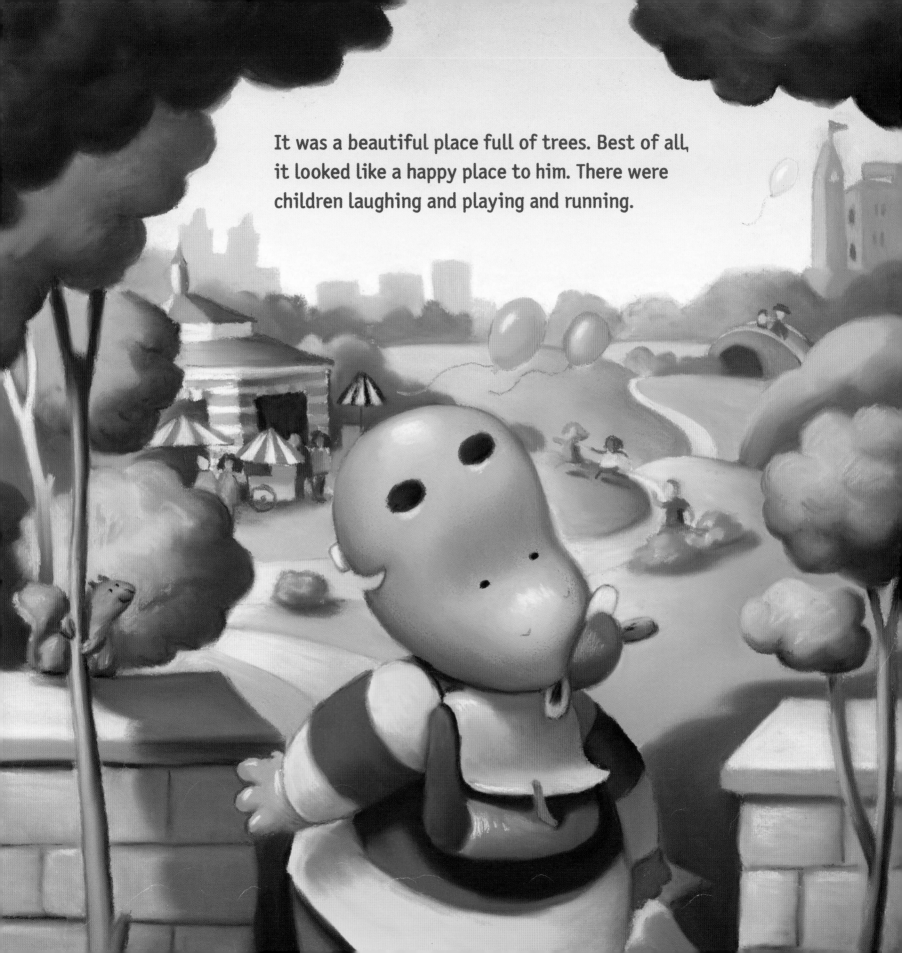

It was a beautiful place full of trees. Best of all, it looked like a happy place to him. There were children laughing and playing and running.

He stopped at a playground. It was full of children, on swings and on seesaws and in the sandbox.

"You're too big to play in the sandbox!" he heard someone say.
"And you're green!"

Greenie's feelings were hurt. They had told him he was too big
and too green and just too different, which made him really sad.

Greenie walked over to the seesaw and tried to find a friend. One mother explained to him that if he rode the seesaw, it would never get off the ground. He was just too big.

Greenie tried the swings next and found he couldn't fit into the seats. And to make everything worse, he hadn't made a single friend.

Finally, he was walking slowly out of the playground when he saw a little boy sitting on a bench alone. Greenie didn't even say hello. He didn't want to scare the boy, since he seemed to scare everyone else.

Suddenly, he heard a voice behind him.

It was the boy from the bench!

"Hi, where are you going?" the boy asked him.

"I don't know. No one will let me play in the sandbox," he explained to the boy.

"Why not?"

"They say I'm too big and too green. No one wants to ride the seesaw with me, and I tried the swings this morning, and all of them were too small."

"What's your name?" asked the boy.

"I'm Greenie," he answered.

"I'm Charlie. My favorite color is
green!" the boy said with a smile.
"Would you like to try the seesaw?"
    "I'd love it! Do you think we could?
I'm a lot bigger than you are."

While Charlie and Greenie went together to the seesaw, Charlie told him how it could work.

They tried it, and it *did* work!

Just then Charlie's babysitter came over to them. "*Who* is that?" she asked.

"He's my friend," Charlie said simply.

They stopped for a minute at the sandbox on the way out, and Greenie sat down in the soft sand with a delighted expression.

"I love sand," Greenie said happily.

"I'll bring two pails and some shovels tomorrow," Charlie promised, and with that Greenie followed him out and walked him to the edge of the park.

"See you tomorrow," Greenie said.

The next day Charlie came back to the playground.

He was happy to see his friend Greenie. He had never seen anyone as beautiful as the green hippopotamus.

They rode the seesaw again, and just as he had promised, Charlie had brought two pails and two shovels, and they made a beautiful castle.

As Charlie looked at Greenie in the afternoon sun, he knew just how special Greenie was and how lucky he was to have him as a friend.

Greenie told Charlie that someone had called him a monster again that day. He hated it when people did that. Sometimes it made him wonder if it were true. It was hard looking different from everyone else.

"Of course you're not a monster," Charlie reassured him. "That's the silliest thing I've ever heard. You just look different, that's all. And you're bigger. Regular hippopotamuses don't look very nice in gray. You're much better in green."

Charlie didn't run away from him. He didn't call him a monster. He wasn't afraid of him. He thought Greenie was beautiful, and he was proud to be his friend. And Greenie was just as proud.

And with that, Greenie was the happiest hippo in the world, no matter how big he was, or how green he was, or how different. And he knew as he fell asleep that he and Charlie would be best friends forever.